Eating Ice Cream with

Eating Ice Cream with a Werewolf

by *Phyllis Green*
illustrations by *Patti Stren*

A YEARLING BOOK

Published by
Dell Publishing
a division of
The Bantam Doubleday Dell Publishing Group, Inc.
666 Fifth Avenue
New York, New York 10103

ISBN: 0-440-42182-9

Reprinted by arrangement with Harper & Row, Publishers, Inc.
Printed in the United States of America

July 1985

10 9 8 7

CW

for Lyn and Paul
P.G.

---

for david (of course) and for richard
from sweet petunia
P.S.

CHAPTER

1

"Brad, have you exercised today?"

That's my mother calling. I'm Brad. Brad Gowan. I'm twelve years old and I'm in my room because I hate exercise. If I'm very quiet, Mom will think I'm jogging around the block.

We live in Madison, Wisconsin, in a ranch house in the Faircrest neighborhood and I go to Jefferson

Middle School, seventh grade. This is our second year in Wisconsin. We have also lived in Pennsylvania and Delaware and I was born in California.

My dad is a battery salesman, but mostly he is an ex-athlete. Whenever we come to a new town, right off he makes a splash. We no sooner got here to Madison than people were buzzing about the famous-twenty-years-ago all-American football great, Keith Gowan. I don't know how it leaks out so fast. *I* never tell anyone. Sometimes I suspect my dad calls the newspapers. Before you know it, people are inviting Dad to lunch and Mom and Dad to parties, and they are in the thick of the party people.

It's hard for me to live with my father's reputation. He thrives in his ex-glory and expects me to follow in his footsteps. But there are three things I violently dislike:

1. participating in sports
2. exercise
3. fresh air

Other than that, my dad is pretty nice. And I know he has problems too, like his tummy that is trying to bulge out of its well-trained muscles. He wants to keep in shape, but each year it gets harder. He studies the beer cans and says to them, "And you don't help either."

I can imagine how uncomfortable it is for him at parties when people ask about his family and what football team his son is on. I don't know how he answers, but I think it must be rough and I'm really sorry. It probably makes him sad. I would like to make him happy with me. But I don't know if I can join a team or if I will just think about it.

Mom tries to help Dad out by encouraging me to do active things. I have to take tennis and swimming lessons at Parkcrest Pool, things like that.

KEITH GOWAN

exact location of his bald spot

a little grey over his ears

MY DAD

MY DAD'S STOMACH

But my parents are o.k. My father is in pretty good shape if you overlook his stomach and his bald spot and the gray hair over his ears. My mother looks forty, which is what she is.

"It's better than looking ninety," she says.

She has sprinkled gray in her brown hair and a face that wants to smile all the time, even in serious circumstances. She is definitely not glamorous, but we like her. Her name is Lois Gowan. It is also

LOIS GOWAN (alias LOIS WELLINGTON)

sprinkled grey

the rest of her hair is brown

a face that wants to smile all the time

MY MOM

she may be a failure as a housewife...but she's a success as an author

MY MOM'S TYPEWRITER

Lois Wellington. Mom is a free-lance writer and uses Lois Wellington as a pen name. She has sold about five stories.

Mom is pretty casual about housework and laundry. Dad has to remind her when he is out of clean shorts to wear to work. When she sells a story, she throws her arms into the air and exclaims, "I may be a failure as a housewife, but I'm a success as an author!" One of Mom's favorite plots is about a frail boy who perseveres and after a shattering adventure becomes an athlete with rippling muscles. Who can she possibly be thinking of???

My sister, Nancy, is four years old. She has muscles and is very big for four. I call her Fat Nancy. She is stronger than me. I remember when she was

the kid had muscles at two

FAT NANCY

OUR DOG PEP

two years old I was supposed to take a toy away from her that belonged to our dog, Pep, because she was putting it in her mouth. It was in the shape of a hot dog in a bun, and it was made of hard rubber and had Pep's bassett-hound slobbers all over it. I grabbed it to take it away and we had a real tug-of-war. She had such muscles at age two! She almost pulled me into the playpen. I screamed for Mom, who gave

Nancy a cookie, and then Nancy gave me Pep's toy. I always had respect for Nancy after that.

It's my job to read Nancy stories at bedtime. She likes me to read to her. And we talk. It's fun.

GRAM SUMMERS

C H A P T E R

2

I have three grandparents. Gram Summers is known for her chocolate-chip cookies. When Gramp died, three years ago, she first cried her eyes out and then she got a job delivering mail. She loves it and Mom and Dad tell everyone what gumption she has.

"Hello from your mailperson," she writes on her postcards.

She lives in Idaho. She and Gramp were born there. It's amazing to her how we move around the country so much. But I guess everybody does nowadays, so there's not much point in thinking about it.

When I see Gram Summers, she grabs me and says, "You're going to be an interesting man."

I think that's because she likes me. I know I'm not that interesting a boy.

I like my other grandparents, the Gowans, too, even though they are sort of stiff and formal and it seems as if we are always meeting for the first time. My mother laughs and says, "They never thought the marriage would work. Any day they expect Keith to run home."

(used to be until I moved from Delaware)
MY BEST FRIENDS

Darryl and Donald

When we lived in Delaware, I had two best friends. Darryl and Donald. They are twins. They never went anywhere without each other, so we were all three best friends.

Here I don't have a best friend. I have some possibility friends. Kids at school talk to me and we fool around. But nobody comes over after school. It isn't always easy when you move a lot, but I guess I'll survive.

The person I walk to school with is Julie Bugle. She is sixteen and lives next door. I'm not sure why Julie Bugle walks to school with me. I know I look out the window and rush out, as I see her go over the rail fence, and call, "Hey, Julie, hi."

you can't tell
from this
drawing but
Julie is 5' 10"

Julie Bugle

She waits for me to climb the fence, and then we walk to school together. She goes to Memorial High School and she is a junior. Our schools are separated by a parking lot.

Julie is very tall, five feet ten. She says she is

taller than most of the boys. She doesn't have a boy-friend yet. She says, "I'm the sweetest sixteen you can think of." Her hair is dark and cut short.

Julie likes languages. She takes French III. When I found out Julie liked French, I bought myself a French-English dictionary. Sometimes we talk French on the way to school and sometimes Julie tells me funny things that her mother and father say or do. I call the Bugles the laugh-a-minute family.

When I jog, I see another big kid on the block. Gray Sonderman, a senior in high school, is usually playing basketball in his driveway. He likes to talk to me. Mostly, he asks me questions about Julie. He always wants to know, "What's Julie doing tonight?"

GRAY SONDERMAN

what's Julie doing tonight?

soon to be a famous general

Gray wants to go to West Point Military Academy. In the meantime he plays war games. He usually "captures" the Parkcrest Pool. But once he captured my sister's sandbox.

I said, "Why don't you do something worthwhile, like take over the State Capitol?"

Anyhow, it's fun to know a kid who may someday be a famous general.

Here are some things I like. I like stocks, as in stocks and bonds. When I get birthday money, I buy a share. I own one General Motors share and three of American Airlines. I like to read the stock pages of the newspaper.

I also like airplanes. I draw them and I read about them. I study all the different kinds. I pretty much know each one. I love the new ones! They are like wild and beautiful birds! I cut them out of the newspaper and pin them on my bulletin board. I like to fly too. I really like to fly. I think I'll be a pilot.

My father brings home old airline books from his office. They are the airline schedules, and I love to read them and figure out trips. My mother will make up pretend trips and I tell her what time her flight leaves and arrives, what type of aircraft she will be flying on, the name of the airline, and if they will serve her a lunch. Maybe I'll be a travel agent. Or I could be a stockbroker.

Or an inventor. When Nancy and my toilet went kaflooey, I fixed it with a piece of coat hanger and Mom didn't have to call the plumber. Maybe I'll be a plumber, because I also fixed the cold-water faucet in the laundry room when it wouldn't shut off.

BERMUDA

MOM and DAD

CHAPTER

3

One night last month Dad came home with the news that he was going on a business trip.

"It's quick notice, I know," he said. "But the boss decided, and well, what could I do?"

Mother gathered up her writings, tablets, rejection slips and record books. She writes on the kitchen table, so when Dad appears she frantically begins to throw our dinner together.

"Brad, you set the table. Nancy, get the napkins," Mom said.

"Get me a beer, Brad," my father said.

"Nancy, quit throwing napkins all over the floor!" I said.

"Where are you going, Keith?" Mom asked.

"Bermuda," Dad answered.

My mother almost fainted. "Bermuda!" she gasped. "That's where we spent our honeymoon." Her voice sounded like *How could you? How could you go without me?*

"Here, Dad." I handed him the beer. "Look, I twisted the cap off with my cute little set of rippling muscles."

SUPER KID

notice my cute little set of rippling muscles

— 14 —

"Don't look so sad," Dad said. "I told my secretary to get two tickets. Do you think you can get that Phoebe Hadley to baby-sit the kids on this short notice?"

"When shall I tell her to be here?" Mom shouted.

"Friday," Dad said.

"That's two days!" Mom said, dropping the macaroni-and-cheese leftovers on the counter and running to hug Dad.

"Not Phoebe Hadley," I protested. "She almost drowned me once and the next time I ended up in the hospital because of her. She always has a hobby she wants to try out on me. Anyone, but *not* Phoebe Hadley!"

I clutched my throat and staggered around the kitchen. Nancy handed me a napkin.

My mother screamed, "I don't have a thing to wear!"

Dad laughed. "You can buy whatever you need when we get there. Wear your red pantsuit on the plane." Dad is crazy about Mom's red pantsuit.

My tongue hung out the side of my mouth. "I'll probably be dead when you get back," I mumbled.

"I'll phone Phoebe right now," my mother said.

I got down on my knees in front of the telephone. "Anyone but Phoebe," I pleaded. "I haven't made out a will yet."

Mom called. Phoebe accepted.

Mom and Dad were talking about Bermuda and I couldn't get a word in edgewise. I decided to try Dad's favorite subject, sports.

"Hey, Dad, I played a little basketball today over at school."

"How many baskets did you make?"

"Three."

"That's good. Overhand or underhand?"

"Well, underhand."

"I've told you a thousand times. Girls shoot underhand. Shoot like a man."

"O.k.," I said. "I'll be in my room, Mom. Call me when dinner's ready."

At seven-thirty (Fat Nancy's bedtime) I had a few books ready to read to her. She looked sleepy. Her pink pajamas have ballerinas on them.

"Hey," I said, "what do you want to hear tonight? *Macbeth*? *A Midsummer-Night's Dream*? or *The Three Little Pigs*?"

"Pigs pigs pigs!" Nancy said.

"Great great great," I said. "Once upon a time there were three three three little pigs pigs pigs."

At the end of the story, when the wolf got cooked in the boiling pot, Nancy's eyes were half closed and her eyeballs were rolling around. I pulled the light-green blanket up to her chin.

"Hey, Fat Nancy," I whispered. "We're in for a great time. You probably don't remember that baby-sitter, Phoebe Hadley. Phoebe always has a hobby. Like once she was studying lifesaving and she made me go swimming every day and you know I hate water. She'd throw me in the deep end, then jump in and save me. I drank a whole swimming pool that week. Once she was studying first aid. She tied me up in so many bandages and slings and knots, she had to take me to a hospital, where a doctor cut them off. You remember me with all those bandages?"

Nancy started to snore.

Snore, Snore
Snore, Snore
Snore, Snore

"Well, sleep tight, you chubby rascal. You'll need all the rest you can get."

CHAPTER

4

Thursday, going to school, I told Julie about Phoebe.

"She tied me up in bandages once. She said it was a first-aid course. But I'm not so sure. I think she meant to do away with me."

"That's horrible!" Julie said. "She sounds like a monster."

"Well, it wasn't exactly that bad," I admitted.

"All the time she was tying me up with splints and bandages and fake tourniquets, we were giggling. It was when we were done and she couldn't undo the bandages that we got worried. She had to hand feed me, then take me to St. Mary's emergency room and have a doctor cut the bandages off. When Phoebe· explained it was practice for a first-aid course, even the doctor laughed with us."

"You do like to exaggerate, Brad," Julie said in a teasing way. "She's probably very nice."

"Well, did I tell you she kept throwing me into Parkcrest Pool and tried to drown me?"

"Brad, I'm not going to listen to you!"

"Do you know Gray Sonderman?" I asked. I finally asked! Gray had been begging me for weeks to ask her that.

Julie sniffed. "Is he the senior that goes around saluting the teachers?"

"Could be," I said. "He wants to go to West Point."

"That must be him," Julie decided.

"He wants to know what you're doing tonight."

"Why does he want to know that?" Julie asked, slightly exasperated.

"I don't know. What are you doing tonight?"

"Washing my hair," Julie said.

"Hey, me too!" I shouted.

After school that day I watched my mother pack her green suitcase.

"I don't have a thing to wear," she said.

She put in lots of things.

"Of course when we went there on our honeymoon, I had all the right clothes. But I had months to prepare and decide. It was a wonderful honeymoon." She stopped packing and looked at me. "Have we talked about sex yet?" she asked.

the famous sex talk

"No."

"Well," she said, sighing, "remind me to do that when we get back from Bermuda."

"Want me to close the suitcase for you?" I said.

"You're twelve," she said. "If you ever have any questions, just ask. You can ask Dad and me anything, o.k.?"

I nodded, then when she wasn't looking, I crossed my eyes.

"Oh, wait, I forgot my yellow tennis shoes. We might rent those motorbikes."

I couldn't picture my mother on a motorbike. She put in the yellow tennis shoes and I closed the suitcase.

"I hope you have fun," I said, turning the key and handing it to her.

She messed up my hair. "You too, honey. And you will remember to exercise? And help Phoebe with Nancy?"

"I will."

At her bedtime, Nancy handed me the Mother Goose book and I read several verses. They were sort of catchy. The only thing they seemed to do for Nancy was make her sleepy.

"Hey, before you nod, let's talk a minute," I said. "Phoebe Hadley will come tomorrow while I'm at school. I hope you'll be o.k. when I get home. Do you think you can protect yourself? Yeah, you're pretty tough.

"What do you suppose Phoebe will have for a hobby this time? I don't know if you can remember the time she kept throwing me in the Parkcrest Pool and then jumping in to save me. But surely you remember the bandages? I think she put a splint on your leg."

NANCY SNORING AGAIN
(AS USUAL WHEN I START TALKING)

Nancy snored.

"The time I almost hate to think about was when she was learning to 'cook for crowds.' Remember, she was thinking of opening a catering service? She brought this *Cooking for Crowds* cookbook and she rented those enormous pots and pans? One night for dinner she made enough spaghetti to serve seventy-five people? Remember how long it took for the garbage disposal to eat it? Then the afternoon she baked twenty blueberry pies and we passed them out to the neighbors? And remember when I accidentally poured that big pan of cookie dough on you and we almost made a Nancy cookie?"

remember when I almost made a Nancy cookie?

Nancy rolled over and started to suck her thumb.

"How about the time she was taking judo lessons and flipped the mailman when he handed her the mail? You don't remember that either? I bet the mailman remembers it. I never saw him again. He must have gotten a new route."

I fixed Nancy's blanket and turned out the light.

Later, when I was washing my hair, using more and more shampoo and building a skyscraper of bubbles on my head, I thought of Julie Bugle. *We are both washing our hair,* I thought.

Phoebe is in charge of me and Nancy and ⟶ I'm in charge of Pep

C H A P T E R

5

Friday, day of departure.

It felt like Dad was staring at me all through breakfast.

"Have fun in Bermuda," I said.

Dad cleared his throat. "Brad?"

"Yes."

"Phoebe is in charge of you and Nancy."

"I know."

"And you're in charge of Pep."

"Oh, o.k.," I said.

"Feed him and take him for walks," Mom said.

"O.k."

"Read Nancy!" Nancy said. "Read Nancy! Read Nancy!" Nancy doesn't contribute much to our conversations.

"Now, Brad," Dad said, looking very serious. "You don't dislike Phoebe, do you?"

"No," I assured him. "Oh, you mean the other day? I was just being goofy. Honest."

"I thought so," Dad said. "Actually you were very funny carrying on all over the kitchen."

"I was?"

"Yes, I told the men at the office you might one day be a comedian on TV."

"You did?"

I thought he was going to shake my hand then, and maybe he was, but instead he got out of his chair and came over and hugged me. Then he hugged Nancy.

It really felt good, and I thought maybe even if

I'm not a jock, maybe he really likes me. Except at that moment I wished I was a jock.

Mom started to cry when I went to school. I wish she wouldn't do that because my eyes are copycats.

"I'll miss you so much," she whispered.

"I know," I whispered back. "Have fun."

"Phoebe will be here when you get home from school."

"O.k."

At school Mr. Hefner, my science teacher, cracked a few jokes. He kept sniggering. That's how we knew what he said was supposed to be funny. Then in gym we had coed gym and it was a dance. I asked this girl, Meredith Jones, to dance, twice. Then I asked her best friend, Jeanne Talbot, so nobody would guess I like Meredith. Meredith has freckles and braces. Ever since she got braces, she has talked funny.

I like Merideth

but ever since she got braces she talks funny

I guess she can't help it. I don't know if she likes me. She might.

INTRODUCING PHOEBE

lavender
jump suit

and
matching
cape

my
tote
bag

THE ONE AND ONLY
MOD, PART-TIME WITCH

When I got home from school, Phoebe Hadley was there. The first thing I did was to see if Nancy was tied up in white bandages. She wasn't.

"Hi, Phoebe."

"Hi, friend," Phoebe said.

Phoebe had on a lavender jump suit with a matching cape. It touched the floor and bumped along behind her. She had never dressed like that before. I hoped she hadn't taken up dressmaking. I could just picture her trying out all the weird costumes on me! That would be a real Phoebe Hadley *thing*. But that wasn't her hobby this time.

"I'm a part-time witch," she said. "I study witch-craft. I cast spells."

"You don't look like a witch," I said. "Witches wear black."

"I'm a mod, part-time witch." Phoebe flung the lavender cape about her shoulders and swooped around the living room.

"Where's your cat?" Fat Nancy asked.

Phoebe's green eyes blinked. "I thought you might ask that."

Phoebe slunk over to a big purple tote bag. She unzipped it and pulled out a big black cat. She held it by the tail. It didn't meow. It was a stuffed toy.

"You've got to do better than that!" I said.

Phoebe threw the cat on the sofa. "Well," she said, smiling, "I tried, but I'm allergic to cat fur."

"Doesn't that automatically make you a failure as a witch? Or can you fly on a broom?" I asked.

She slithered over to the blue chair and sat down.

She put her head in her hands. "I'm afraid of heights," she said.

"You must be able to do something!"

Her face came up smiling. "I cast spells," she said.

"Can you prove it?"

Phoebe shrugged her shoulders. "I'm here, aren't I? That was my first spell. I wanted to get your parents off on a trip so I could come over here and you could help me practice my witchcraft."

"I think my dad's boss did that." I said.

"Did he?" she asked. "It was real short notice, wasn't it? Maybe that's because I only thought of it this week. Then, zammo, I cast a spell, and it happens!"

Nancy clapped her hands. "Say it. Say it, Pebe."

Phoebe rolled her eyes mysteriously. "I'll say it softly because I don't want to cast the spell again. Come sit here on the floor and I'll say it."

Nancy and I sat down on the floor and looked up at Phoebe. Her brown tangled hair was fluffed all over her head and she did look sort of witchy. She looked at a book in her hands and began to chant.

"Lizards try to love your mothers.
  Four green spoons and a bunch of brothers.
  Float a boat. Eat a goat.
  Wigs. Pigs. Eels. Seals. SNAKES!"

Nancy began to cry.

"I think it scared her," I said.

Phoebe swooped Nancy up into her arms. "Let's go into the kitchen and I'll conjure up a witch's snack," she said.

We had Twinkies out of a box on the counter and milk from the refrigerator. Wow, real witchcraft.

Phoebe winked at me. "Brad, I'll show you more witchcraft later. I don't want to scare Nancy."

Even though Phoebe was with us, it was still my job to read Nancy her bedtime story.

"What's Mommy doing now, Brad?" she asked.

"Probably having fun," I said.

"Oh," Nancy said.

She picked *Snow White* for me to read. By the time the prince planted his kisser on the rosy lips of Snow White, Nancy was almost asleep.

"Well, kid," I said, "it looks as though Phoebe

is a part-time witch who goes around casting spells. What will she think of next? Mom and Dad will be gone for a week. I hope when they get home Phoebe hasn't turned us into frogs. And if she offers you an apple, don't eat it. Good night, you little fatty."

WHAT IF PHOEBE TURNS US INTO FROGS?

GUESS WHICH ONE IS NANCY?

CHAPTER

Phoebe was reading her book on casting spells when I finished with Nancy.

"What's it called? Where'd you get it?" I asked.

"*Dr. Curmudgeon's Book of Magic*," Phoebe answered. "The secondhand bookstore next to me went out of business. They practically gave books away. I bought this for twenty-five cents. I thought we could have some fun with it."

"You mean cast some spells together?"

"Exactly," Phoebe said.

Phoebe told me all about herself the first time she baby-sat us. She is from Philadelphia, but she lives in Madison now. She has a plant shop on State Street where she sells plants. It's called Fortunes & Fernery because for a while she was telling people's fortunes there with a deck of cards. It didn't cost anything. If they bought a plant, she would throw in a fortune for free. But she told me she got scared because so many of the fortunes started coming true. People were depending on her to make important decisions for them with a deck of cards! It got to be too much for Phoebe. She threw her cards into the back of a yellow garbage truck. She watched it crunch and swallow them. Now she only sells plants.

Of course she has this baby-sitting agency on the side, which is how my mother got hold of her in the first place. If she gets a good baby-sitting job, she closes the plant shop and sticks a sign on the door that says, "Back in five minutes." Sometimes she is gone from the shop for weeks at a time, but she always stops in to water the plants. Sometimes the bookstore man next door waters them for her.

Phoebe is twenty-seven years old. She went to the University of Wisconsin—Madison. She graduated too, but she didn't want to get a regular job and earn lots of money. Her parents are rich. Sometimes she'll say wryly, "I was a child of affluence." Anyhow, lots of money and money talk upset her.

"I just want to be happy," she'll say. "There are

fashionable jewelery

←fashionable dress

←fashionable shoes

little Miss Post-Debutante

lots of things I want to do in the world. I want to do them all. I won't go home and be little Miss Post-Debutante."

I think her parents have a hard time accepting her dinky plant shop on State Street. She sleeps in back on an Army cot.

"They picture me in a plumpy canopy with maids and butlers and chauffeurs. They can't understand that is not *me*!"

State Street has lots of interesting shops and restaurants and a movie. It begins at the State Capitol building on the square (which is the center of Madison) and goes down to the University campus. You always see lots of students walking or riding bicycles down State Street. There are record shops, sports equipment shops, bicycle shops, gift, shoe, dress and import shops. There's a music shop and a luggage shop, several bookstores and of course Phoebe's Fortunes & Fernery in the tiny shop squeezed between the secondhand bookstore and Beatrice's Beauty Parlor.

"What's the story on the bookstore?" I asked Phoebe.

"Oh, it's rather complicated. He's gone out of

business, sold his shop. He's going to marry his first wife. Actually remarry her. Of course he has to divorce his third wife first. The first wife that he's going to remarry won't live anywhere but New York City, which is why they got divorced in the first place, so now he has decided to live in New York."

"What kind of store is it now?" I asked.

Karen Kuddly (can you believe her name?)

"A dancing school. Karen Kuddly's dancing school. She's a darling girl, though a bit fluttery. You can be walking down the street with her when suddenly she executes a tour jeté. Or she might start running and leaping. She often does ballet exercises on parking meters. It's rather startling when you're

— 38 —

trying to carry on a conversation. But she is pleasant and is looking after my shop while I'm here with you and Nancy."

I picked up *Dr. Curmudgeon's Book of Magic*. "Do you suppose any of this mumbo-jumbo works?"

"I'm quite sure it doesn't," Phoebe said. "But the spells are rather fun to read."

"What's a good one?" I asked.

"I rather liked the barnyard spell," Phoebe said. "Let's see, here it is on page twenty-four. 'If you want a barnyard to appear, cast the following spell.' Should I read it?" she asked.

"Sure. Nothing will happen," I said.

"All right," Phoebe said. "Here goes.

Scrape the barrel. Scrape the pan.
Let the pig loose, and grab a fan.
Swirl. Twirl. Fish. Stop. SCREAM."

I looked around the room. "Well, that was a big deal," I said. "I thought we'd have pigs and cows and horses running all around."

Phoebe laughed. "And wouldn't it be a mess if we did?" she said. "Can you imagine?"

I paged through the book. "Let's see what other

spells we can cast." I read, "Igloo spell, deserted is-
land spell, monster spell, pirate spell, werewolf spell,
Florida spell."

"What's that?" Phoebe said. "Did you hear something?"

"What?"

"I think Nancy is calling."

Phoebe ran to the hallway. "Nancy, did you call
me?"

"Yes," Nancy said. "There's a big chicken on my
bed!"

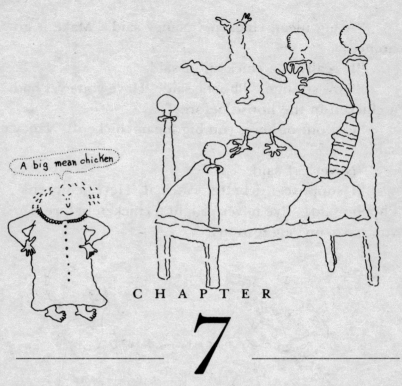

CHAPTER

7

For a moment Phoebe and I stared at each other, then we ran to Nancy's bedroom. There wasn't a big chicken on her bed. It was an ordinary-sized chicken, but it sure was a chicken!

"It's a chicken!" I said.

"Yes," Phoebe said. "A chicken."

"A big mean chicken," Nancy said. "Make it go home."

"It really is a chicken," I said.

"How strange," Phoebe said. "Have you ever had a chicken in the house before?"

"Get out of here, you big mean chicken!" Nancy said.

"Never!" I said.

"I suppose I'd better catch it. Here, chicken!" Phoebe said. "I've never caught a chicken before. Do you have any suggestions?"

I shrugged my shoulders. "The best thing to do, I would say, would be to sneak up from behind it, put your hands out and grab."

"If I get pecked to death," Phoebe said, "please give my regards to your parents."

"I hate you, chicken!" Nancy said.

"Here, little chicken!" Phoebe got hold of the chicken on her sixth try. The chicken squawked. I went to open the window.

"Oh look, it is open," I said. "Maybe that's how it got in. Maybe it flew in."

"Brad, do you see me?" Phoebe asked. "I am holding a chicken. It is squawking. This is a squawking chicken. Please don't give me an analysis of the window. Please move out of the way so I can drop the squawking chicken out."

Phoebe held the chicken over the windowsill and let go. It sort of bumped onto the grass, then stood up and walked around.

"Quick, close the window," Phoebe said. "Now lock it."

I did.

"Now, Nancy dear," Phoebe said, "go back to sleep. Everything is fine."

"Big fat mean chicken," Nancy cried. "I was going to punch it."

"Yes," Phoebe said, "now go back to sleep."

We tiptoed from Nancy's room.

I was going to punch it

"That was weird," I said. "Eerie. Impossible. Unbelievable."

"A coincidence," Phoebe said.

"Chickens live in barnyards," I said.

"It had to be one of life's strange coincidences. I don't for a minute believe that—"

"Let's try casting another spell, then," I said.

Phoebe didn't say anything.

"It's just a book," I said. "There are no such things as magic spells. There's probably no such person as Dr. Curmudgeon. You aren't really a part-time witch. We both know that."

"Of course we do," Phoebe said. "And there are lots of farms down Mineral Point Road, not far from here, any one of which could have a runaway chicken."

"Then we can cast another spell?"

"Oh, sure!" Phoebe said. She smiled. "We can't let a coincidence spoil our evening."

We paged through *Dr. Curmudgeon's Book of Magic* and found a spell for a quiet picnic spot.

"What do you suppose that would be?" Phoebe asked.

"Say you're driving your car and you want to find a place to have lunch, you'd point and say, 'There's a nice quiet picnic spot.' " I said.

"Sounds harmless," Phoebe said.

"We could try something exciting like this mountain-climbing expedition spell," I said.

"And have us end up on top of Mount Everest?" Phoebe said.

"You're beginning to believe *Dr. Curmudgeon's Book of Magic*," I teased.

"I'm not!" Phoebe quickly denied. "I just think a nice quiet picnic spot would be better than a mountain-climbing expedition. That's all."

"All right," I agreed.

Phoebe looked around the room dramatically and then began to read the spell.

> *"Pass the pepper. Pass the salt.*
> *What's the commotion all about?*
> *Pull up your socks. Throw out three rocks.*
> *Pickles. Eggs. Peas, please. ANTS!"*

She sort of whispered at first, then her voice got louder, and when she was finished I was thoroughly convinced a quiet picnic spot would just pop out and appear in the middle of the living room. We sat quietly for a minute.

"You sounded real magical," I said. "I thought for sure, you know, for a moment, that something would happen."

"I know what you mean, Brad. I felt it too. But, I guess . . . well, should we try another spell?"

"I'm kind of hungry," I said. "Let's have a snack first. I started to walk to the kitchen. "Can I get you anything?" I asked.

"Whatever you're having," Phoebe answered.

I came back to the living room with two peanut-butter-and-cucumber sandwiches, a bag of potato chips and two iced teas.

"Brad!" Phoebe said. "I thought you said snack, not banquet. I thought you'd bring me an Oreo cookie."

"I didn't have room," I answered. "I'll get some when we finish this."

"Don't bother," Phoebe said. "This is more than I can eat as it is. Why are your shoes wet?" she asked.

I looked at my shoes.

I touched them. "I don't know."

"All right. We must stay calm," Phoebe said, looking very excited. "You have wet feet. Very wet feet. It must be raining in the kitchen. What am I saying?" she gasped.

We ran to the kitchen and I almost slid across the linoleum. There was water on the floor.

"It was the spell!" Phoebe said. "I'm going to throw that book away. I should have known a quiet picnic place is by a stream."

I waded into the laundry room. "You can keep the book, Phoebe. I see what the trouble is. The cold-water faucet is leaking again. I fixed this faucet before. I'll go down to the basement and turn the water off.

It fills up the laundry tub and then overflows. See? There's a whole bunch of lint in the drain. I can fix it."

"Oh?" Phoebe said. "A leaky faucet? That's what I thought. As soon as I saw those wet shoes, I said to myself *somewhere there is a leaky faucet.* I'll get some towels and dry up this stream," she said.

"It's water from the faucet," I reminded her.

"Right," she said.

I'm not sure she was convinced.

nancy

me

Pep

phoebe

Fortunes
&
Fernery

ON OUR WAY TO CHECK ON PHOEBE'S SHOP

CHAPTER

8

Saturday morning Phoebe took Nancy and me and also Pep down to State Street to check on her shop. She drives an orange Volkswagen that says Fortunes & Fernery on the sides. Pep stuck his head out the side window and barked at the other cars all the way downtown. He is an obnoxious traveler, as my dad claims. When he is in a car is about the only time he doesn't sleep.

Pep is not so good out of the car on a trip either. Phoebe went right to her shop. Nancy and I were supposed to tie Pep to the parking meter, but he wouldn't cooperate. Pep doesn't like to be tied to parking meters. Both Nancy and I had to tug and pull so there was enough room to slip his leash around the meter. Then Pep tripped Nancy. She fell and got her elbows dirty. Nancy doesn't like her elbows dirty, so she punched Pep in the side and he bit a bicycle going by. The man on the bicycle lurched, and he and the bike fell into a bunch of university students walking past. In the confusion, Nancy and I ran toward State Street and Fortunes & Fernery.

The door was closed when we got there, but we could sure hear Phoebe was in there. She was really mad at someone named Bill. Nancy stared at me, her eyes wide open.

I can't trust you Bill!

"I can't trust you, Bill!" we heard Phoebe yell. "I leave you alone for five minutes and you are up to something. I distinctly told you to leave Imogene and Ida alone. But do you do that? Oh no! You have your own ideas. Well, I don't know what I'm going to do with you. You are impossible!"

"What's wrong, Brad?" Nancy whispered.

"I don't know," I said. "She's mad at someone named Bill."

"Look at poor Imogene," Phoebe shrieked. "She's absolutely crushed! Bill, you are a beast."

"Do you want to peek in?" Nancy asked.

I shook my head no.

"I could punch Bill for Pebe," Nancy said.

"No, Nancy," I said.

"You're nothing but a hulking monster, Bill. Let's face it, if I could think of a way to kill you, I think I would be tempted to do it. I mean, look at Ida. She's a perfect wreck from just being close to you."

We could hear Phoebe walking through the store. She opened the shop door and looked at us.

"What are you two doing out here?" she asked. "Why didn't you just walk in?"

"No!" Nancy said.

"We don't really want to," I added.

"Listen," Phoebe said, folding her arms across her waist, "would it be all right if I brought Bill home with us?"

"Are you going to murder him at our house?" Nancy asked.

"Murder him? Oh, no," Phoebe said, laughing. "I just like to scare him. Come, I want you to meet him."

"Don't go in there, Brad," Nancy said. "I don't like Bill."

"You're going to love Bill!" Phoebe said. "I'll bring him out."

THE REMNANTS
of IDA

INTRODUCING BILL
(alias hulking monster)

THE REMNANTS
of IMOGENE

She soon returned with a giant-sized geranium plant. "Here's Bill," she said. "He's a little ungainly."

"This is Bill?" I said.

"He's horrible to my other plants. He's so big and he pushes them around and tries to grab all the sunlight for himself. I think he'll be perfect for your living-room window. He can have all the sunlight to himself and he'll produce lovely red flowers for your family to enjoy. May I bring him home with us?"

Nancy and I looked at each other and giggled. "Sure!" we said.

Bill and Nancy and I went into the shop while Phoebe checked her other plants and talked to them. Ida and Imogene seemed relieved that Bill was going away. Ida is a baby's tears plant and Imogene is an African violet.

We fooled around the shop. Phoebe made some phone calls. Nancy and I played with the cash register. Nancy was a mugger who was robbing the store. She could probably grow up to be a good mugger. She sure talked tough. I gave her all Phoebe's cash. Just pretend, of course.

Phoebe did some dusting. I swept the floor for her. Nancy did nothing—she's pretty good at that.

"Well, my dears, everything seems to be in order. Shall we go home?" Phoebe asked. She picked up Bill. We went out to the sidewalk. Phoebe locked her shop. "Oh," she said, "I want to ask Karen something. Come with me."

She took us and Bill into Karen Kuddly's dance studio. It was a big bare room. There was a wooden rail along one wall and mirrors along the other wall. There was one person in the room doing cartwheels.

"Karen," Phoebe said, "I'd like to get in touch with Nathan. He had this book sale before he left, and I bought a book on magic that, well, I'd like to write to him about. Do you have his New York address?"

KAREN KUDDLY
(believe me she's pretty)

All this time Karen was doing cartwheels. She would get to one end of the room and then she'd cartwheel to the other end. Nancy and I were fascinated. Then she began to talk as she cartwheeled.

"He's changed his name, you know," Karen said.

"It's not Nathan anymore?" Phoebe said.

"His last name. He changed it to his first wife's name. It was part of her requirements."

"Well, that's understandable," Phoebe said. "Not everyone could stand being Mrs. Nathan Hale twice."

"McGraw," Karen said, whirling. Then suddenly she stood up. "One hundred fifty!" she exclaimed.

She was pretty. She had a black beauty mark on her chin and lots of black globby stuff on her eyelashes. She had long black hair and she wore a pale-pink leotard.

"Nathan McGraw," Phoebe repeated as she wrote it down on Bill's clay pot.

Karen found Nathan's address in her purse. Phoebe copied it.

"Thanks, Karen," Phoebe said. "I do want to find out about this magic book. We were casting some spells and some things happened—well, I won't bother you about it, but thanks for taking care of my plants. They look fine. Remember now, I want to do a favor for you in return."

Karen smiled. "Have you ever thought of taking tap dancing lessons? I only have two students so far," she said, shrugging.

"Oh, sure!" Phoebe said. "I'll be your third student as soon as Brad and Nancy's parents get home."

"When will they get home?" Nancy asked me. "Shh," I whispered.

We walked down the street, gathered up Pep and put him in the backseat with Bill. Nancy and I rode home in the front seat with Phoebe. Nancy held on to my hand.

"Mom and Dad will be home before you know it," I assured her.

We set Bill in the living-room window, then we went to the kitchen to eat lunch.

CUTE LITTLE DUCKS WE FED

CHAPTER

9

On Sunday, Phoebe said we could take a picnic to Lake Wingra. It is one of Nancy and my favorite things to do. We eat at the lake and these cute ducks swim by and we throw bread at them. Sometimes they come up to the grass to eat. Sometimes they come as close as six inches away from our feet! Then when we are tired of the ducks, we walk across the street to Vilas

Zoo. There are lots of animals there. It's a nice zoo.

The first thing we decided to do was to leave Pep at home. Sometimes he is a pest. I don't think the ducks at the lake like him.

I helped Phoebe pack our picnic. Nancy thought she was helping too, but all she did was put the napkins in the bag. It took her about ten minutes to count three napkins. She counts like this: 1, 5, 8, 2, 40. I bet the kindergarten teacher can hardly wait to get hold of her.

1 – 5 – 8 – 2 – 40

it takes Nancy about ten minutes to count three napkins.

We made egg-salad sandwiches and we also took potato chips, fudge cookies, cider, paper cups and an old blue tablecloth.

"Ready?" Phoebe said.

"Ready," I answered, smiling.

"Bread!" Nancy said.

We had forgotten the bread for the ducks! So we put that in the bag too. We got into the orange Volkswagen and were on our way.

In about ten minutes we were at the lake. We found an empty picnic table and broke out the lunch. There were two sailboats on the lake. It is a nice small lake. You can't have motorboats on it at all. Only quiet boats.

A whole mess of ducks came to eat our bread. Nancy and I climbed a tree at the edge of the lake. We only climbed to the first notch, but it felt good to sit there and look around.

"I wish I had a camera," Phoebe said. "You both look cute in the tree."

"Zoo," Nancy said.

So we cleaned up our picnic and walked across the street to the zoo. We walked over a couple of wooden bridges and entered the zoo by the elephant enclosure.

There's a baby elephant and two big elephants. They stand by the wall and try to get people to throw them peanuts. Then they pick the peanuts up with their trunks and put the peanuts into their mouths.

We watched them for a while. We didn't have any peanuts. I tried to fool them with twigs. It didn't work.

Phoebe wanted to see the giraffes next, so we walked to their building and enclosure. I like giraffes.

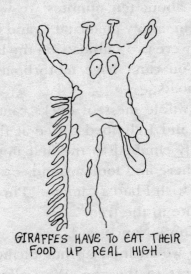

GIRAFFES HAVE TO EAT THEIR
FOOD UP REAL HIGH.

I think they are one of the nicest-looking animals. I like their colors and their long necks and how they are always trying to eat something up real high when most food grows low. They even lick bare tree limbs and fences.

There were some birds in with the giraffes. I

didn't remember seeing them before. They were goofy-looking, and they were acting goofy too. They were really big birds, as tall as me or taller, and they were mostly dark gray and slightly dark green and edged in white. Their beaks were practically a foot long! I don't think even another bird would call them handsome.

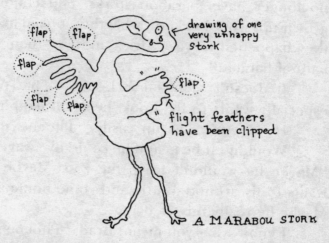

drawing of one very unhappy stork

flight feathers have been clipped

A MARABOU STORK

"They're marabou storks," Phoebe said, reading the sign.

"Look, they want to fly," I said. "See that one? On the rock. He's flapping like mad. But nothing happens."

"His left wing has been clipped. See?" Phoebe said.

I saw an open space on the bottom of his left wing. You could tell feathers should be there, but they weren't.

"They clip the flight feathers," Phoebe said. "Otherwise they would fly away and the zoo would no longer have marabou storks, and children and grown-ups wouldn't know what they looked like unless they happened to visit Africa and saw them in their natural habitat."

"It doesn't seem fair," I said. "That one bird especially wants to fly. Look, he's still flapping."

"He doesn't give up easily," Phoebe admitted.

"Wouldn't it be neat if he could fly away?" I said. "Maybe he wouldn't leave the zoo. Maybe he just wants to fly around a little and come home at night. Maybe he really misses flying."

"I know what you mean, Brad," Phoebe said. "It is a little sad."

"Gee, he's flapping like crazy!"

"He seems to believe he can do it," Phoebe said.

"Boy, I really wish he could," I said. "Don't you,

Phoebe? Don't you wish they hadn't clipped his wings?"

"Seals," Nancy said, pulling Phoebe's arm.

"Fly, Hepzibah, fly!" Phoebe called. "I've named him Hepzibah," she said.

"Flap harder," I urged the big bird.

"C'mon, Hepzibah, you can do it," Phoebe said.

Nancy kicked me in the ankle. "Seals," she said bitterly.

I showed her my fist. "Don't kick me, Nancy," I said.

"Seals," Nancy moaned to Phoebe. "Seals!"

"Oh, all right," Phoebe said. "Brad, we better move on."

"But I wanted to see Hepzibah fly!"

"You've got me wanting it too. But Brad, dear, we know, don't we, that Hepzibah can't fly anymore?"

"I guess."

"So, on to the seals!" Phoebe said.

We walked around the whole zoo. We saw the seals, the lions, the zebras, the camels, the wildebeest, the peacocks. Up by the polar bears I saw Gray Sonderman staring at the Galápagos turtles.

← Gray Sonderman just staring at the turtles waiting to take them as prisoners of war.

"Hey, Gray!" I said. "Did you just capture the zoo? Are you taking the animals as prisoners of war? I see you already have them in cages!"

He turned toward me. "Oh, hi, Brad," he said after a moment.

"Next, the Capitol building," I kidded him.

He sort of smiled. He looked quiet and strange.

I felt embarrassed for teasing him.

"What's the matter?" I said.

"Nothing," he said quickly. "Um, you having a good time at the zoo?" he asked. "It's a nice zoo," he said before I could answer.

"Yeah," I said.

"Well, good seeing you," he said. "I'm headed this way," he said, pointing to the penguins.

That was weird, I thought. Then I heard him call to me.

"How's your doberman pinscher?"

He meant Pep. That's what he calls Pep. "O.k.," I called back. *Well,* I thought, *I guess you can't always feel like joking.* Still, I felt embarrassed.

Believe it or not this is Nancy's favorite animal.

I must have stuck it out around those monkeys for ten smelly minutes.

Our last stop was the monkeys, which is one of Nancy's favorite places. I'm not too fond of the stink. We must have stayed there ten smelly minutes. It's hard to hold your nose that long. Phoebe said it was time to go home.

We went out the way we came in, and as we passed the giraffe and marabou enclosure, I called out, "Fly, Hepzibah!" He was still flapping.

"You can do it," Phoebe added.

NANCY HAVING A DUMB
CONVERSATION ON HER
DUMB PINK TOY PHONE

CHAPTER

10

After dinner Sunday night Nancy about had a temper
tantrum till Phoebe and I promised to play with her
and her pink toy telephone. It is such a dumb toy.
Maybe when I was four I didn't think so. Now I do.

Nancy pretended she was dialing Mom and Dad
in Bermuda.

"Mommy, is that you, Mommy?" Nancy said into

the phone. "What are you doing, Mommy? What is Daddy doing? I'm having fun with Pebe and Brad. I'm not thinking about you. Are you thinking about me? Do you want to come home now? What is Daddy doing now?"

Then Nancy insisted Phoebe talk to them.

"Hello, Gowans!" Phoebe said into the pink toy phone. "Nancy and Brad are being perfect, just perfect! Is Bermuda nice?"

Then it was my turn. I felt it was awfully silly.

"Hello?" Crazily enough, I half expected them to answer me out of Nancy's pink phone. "Are you buying me a T-shirt in Bermuda? What? What's that you say? You want to hang up? Oh, gosh, Nancy. Mom says we have to stop talking now. What a shame. Good-bye, Mom." I handed the phone back to Nancy. "Say good-bye," I coached.

She obediently said good-bye. Then she dialed

(pretend) Gram Summers, Grandfather and Grandmother Gowan, Aunt Lilly, Aunt Connie and Reverend Poggins. Nancy had a fit till I talked to them too. It was a really dumb game, and I was so glad when she had to go to bed.

I read her a couple pages of *Macbeth* for punish-

ME TRYING TO TORMENT MY LITTLE SISTER WITH SHAKESPEARE

ment. She really had it coming, but she seemed too tired to mind. At least she didn't punch me.

I couldn't believe it when I went back to the living room. Phoebe was holding the toy phone in her lap. She looked like she was dialing it. She *was* dialing it.

"What are you doing?" I asked, startled.

"Making a phone call," she said, straight-faced.

I decided to humor her. "Who are you calling?"
I asked.

"My father."

"Oh," I said.

"I just realized it's his birthday. I didn't send a
card or anything. So I better phone him," Phoebe
said.

"On Nancy's pink plastic phone?"

"It's September. This is his birthday. Today,"
Phoebe said. "He's forty-nine. Oh my gosh! Forty-
nine!"

"Is it really his birthday?" I asked.

She put the phone to her ear. "Excuse me, he
just answered. Hello, Daddy! Happy birthday. It's
Phoebe, your daughter. I just called to say have a
lovely birthday. I love you and all that. . . . I'm fine.
And you? And Mother? You're welcome. I was glad
to call. Bye-bye, Daddy."

Phoebe put the phone on its hook and walked

over to Nancy's toy box and dropped it in. Its bell sort of clanged when it hit the other toys.

"What are you doing?" I said. I think my nose was wrinkled up when I said it. It felt wrinkled up.

"Being silly," Phoebe said. "Forget it. It was a joke." She smiled.

"If it's really his birthday, why don't you really call him?" I said.

"Can't," Phoebe said.

"Sure you can. Mom won't mind. Or you could pay her, or whatever."

"It's not that kind of can't. It's I can't because, oh, you don't want to know. It's like a soap opera thing. I can't call him. I can't send him a card."

"Why?"

"He doesn't want anything to do with me till I 'come to my senses.' That's the key phrase in Philadelphia. 'She'll soon come to her senses,' so they say. I never thought these things happened in real life. I don't meet my parents' expectations, and they say they've put up with my foolishness long enough. They won't have anything to do with me till I 'come to my senses.' "

"Have they disowned you?"

"Sort of. Isn't it humorous? I'm twenty-seven and still they treat me like a small child."

"Gee," I said.

"I guess they want to take me back to Philadelphia and clip my wings. Like Hepzibah," she said, laughing. "Hepzibah and I keep flapping!"

PHOEBE AND HEPZIBAH KEEP FLAPPING AWAY

I didn't know what to say. I didn't know if what she said was partly true and partly kidding. It's so hard to tell with Phoebe. Sometimes when she gets serious, I almost think she is teasing.

"Why is it parents who love us so much also burden us with their expectations?" Phoebe said. "Why must we turn out the way they want? Why can't we be ourselves? Why must we be them all over again?"

I began to understand a little bit of what she

meant. "My dad wants me to be athletic because he was," I said.

"The thing that scares me terribly," Phoebe said, "is that someday when I'm broke and depressed I may give up and go back to Philadelphia and confess that I've come to my senses."

"I can't dribble," I said. "My bowling balls head right for the gutter. I can't even shoot pool. I'm horrible at pickup sticks!"

"Well, I try to remember that maybe they had burdens put on them, by *their* parents. Maybe it's a long chain of burdens. I do know if I have children I'll try very hard to let them be the kind of person they want to be. Even if I have a daughter who wants

— 73 —

to be a stuffy little debutante, well, I'll let her, if that's what she wants."

Phoebe was steamed up. I was afraid she was going to talk all evening like she had the night before—then we wouldn't get to try some more magic spells from *Dr. Curmudgeon's Book of Magic*.

"Phoebe, do you want to do some magic spells tonight?"

She brushed some curls away from her eyes. "Oh Brad, dear, you know, I don't feel like it tonight. Let's watch TV."

So we did.

CHAPTER

11

I stood at the back door Monday morning watching for Julie Bugle to come out of her house. When she got to the fence, I opened the door and called, "Hey Julie, hi!"

"Hi, Brad," she called back. "Walk with ya."

I ran out with my book bag slung on my back and climbed over the fence. "Hi," I said.

"You're surviving," Julie observed. "Your baby-sitter hasn't killed you yet."

"She's trying to," I said. "Now she's a part-time witch. She has this book on magic and we're casting spells."

"I bet really terrible things are happening," Julie said, giggling.

"They are! Really," I said.

"Maybe some of the magic is spreading," Julie said. "I got a wish this weekend I've been wishing for ages. I had my first date Saturday night."

"You did?"

DRAWING OF WHAT ALMOST HAPPENED AT SHAR-LEE'S ICE CREAM PARLOR

"Yeah. Your friend, Gray Sonderman. We went to the movies and then to Shar-Lee's Ice Cream parlor. He tried to kiss me good night, but we more or less bumped noses because he surprised me and I turned my head weirdly. I don't know if I like dates or not. We didn't have much to talk about. He kept staring at me."

"Did Gray have a battle plan for getting to Shar-Lee's? Did he capture the building first?" I asked. "Did he shoot first and ask for ice cream later? Did he blow up the soda fountain?"

Julie laughed. "He really does want to be a famous general. But we just had a regular date. Oh, Brad, listen, I know a secret. You won't tell?"

I shook my head no.

"Gray's father . . . well . . . he's sick. Um . . . mentally. I think they're going to have to put him in a home. God, if you tell anyone I'll—"

"I won't tell," I said. "I wouldn't tell that. What kind of person do you think I am?"

"O.k. It was so good to tell you. Gray told me. I guess he had to tell someone. I promised not to tell my parents, but I had to tell someone."

"I won't tell anyone," I said. "Honest."

"Let's change the subject," Julie said. "I'm going to take piano lessons. My first. Mom is looking for a teacher. She got one lady who charges eight dollars for a half-hour lesson whether you are present or absent. My mother told the woman that she thought the price quite high, higher than she intended to pay. The teacher insisted on sending mother a brochure about the lessons. You wouldn't believe the brochure! It tells where the lady went to school, who she studied with, what clubs she belongs to, her philosophy—my mother read it out loud to us at dinner. Well, we just laughed and laughed. Then mother took a red felt-tip pen and wrote across the brochure, 'But have you played for kings?' and mailed it back to the teacher!"

We were almost at our schools. I never do quite understand the Bugle family jokes. But they seem to laugh a lot at dinnertime.

"I might take piano lessons," I said, although I had never thought of it before.

"Well, see you," Julie said.

We waved.

That night, after Nancy went to bed, Phoebe and I got back to *Dr. Curmudgeon's Book of Magic*. Phoebe sat on the sofa, leafing through the pages.

"It's just a book," she kept saying. "Somebody wrote it for fun. As a joke. The little spells don't mean a thing. It's all good fun, just as I thought it would be."

"Find a good spell," I said. I was sitting on the rug in front of Phoebe, anxious for the magic to begin.

"Here's one," she said, her eyes sparkling. "We could turn you into a guppy."

"What?" I said, grabbing the book. I looked at the fish spell.

we could turn you into a guppy

what!!

SUPER KID

Nibble on this and nibble on that.

Nibble on this and nibble on that,
  Just don't nibble on a very fat cat.
  Sit in mud. Chew your cud.
  Funny bones. Warts. Scarecrows. SPIDERS!

"Uh, let's not do that one," I said, quietly. "You know I don't like to swim. There must be something that's more fun."

"Oh, there are lots of fun spells," Phoebe said.

"Here's a spell on shrinking heads, for example."

Yikes!

She began flipping the pages. I breathed easier. Then I got my idea to fool her. I remembered that before Mom went to Bermuda she had bought two quarts of vanilla-fudge ice cream and put them in the freezer. I thought if Phoebe cast a spell for two quarts of vanilla-fudge and then we went to the freezer and saw the two quarts, well, she'd really be panicky over *Dr. Curmudgeon's Book of Magic*!

MY BRILLIANT IDEA

"Phoebe," I said, "let's do something simple, like food. Can *Dr. Curmudgeon* conjure up something to eat?"

"We can try," Phoebe said. "What are you hungry for?"

She was falling for my trap. "Gee," I said. "I'm

kind of hungry for two quarts of vanilla-fudge ice cream."

"Two?" Phoebe said, wrinkling her eyebrows.

"We don't want to be too easy on *Dr. Curmudgeon*," I said.

Phoebe shrugged. "Two quarts of vanilla-fudge ice cream coming up."

She found the page for casting spells for food. "Now quiet," she said. "I have to concentrate." She closed her eyes.

"Two quarts of vanilla-fudge ice cream," she chanted. Then she opened her eyes and read the spell.

> *"Calabash cabbage and Mary Lou Savage.*
> *Tricks. Elastic. Storms and plastic.*
> *VIOLA!"*

She looked at me. "Did you feel it?" she whispered.

"What?" I said, even though I knew what she meant. Something had made me shiver, and I almost felt as though a small earthquake had shaken the house.

"The room moved," Phoebe said. "I would swear it moved." She looked around. "However, I see no vanilla-fudge."

I jumped up. "Let's look in the freezer."

"You look," Phoebe said.

"Why don't you look?" I encouraged her.

"You look," Phoebe said.

That wasn't what I had in mind. I wanted Phoebe to find the ice cream, and I wanted to see the look on her face when she did.

"O.k." I said. I decided I'd get the two quarts out of the freezer, and she still might be surprised when I brought them to the living room.

I went to the freezer, pushed aside the Morton doughnuts, the green beans, hamburger meat, the blueberry pancake mix, broccoli, the hot dogs, the Chinese peapods—*where were the two quarts of vanilla-fudge?* I went through the freezer again. And again. There were four boxes of corn, a ham steak, bagels, three grape Popsicles, an opened package of bacon, one turkey pie dinner, but no ice cream!

"Well?" Phoebe called from the living room.

I put everything back in the freezer. I walked into the living room. "Phoebe, did you eat the ice cream Mom had in the freezer?"

"No," she said. "I'm on a diet."

QUESTION:

COULD A FOUR-YEAR-OLD EAT TWO QUARTS OF ICE CREAM IN FOUR DAYS?

"Then it must have been Nancy," I said. "Could a four-year-old eat two quarts of ice cream in four days? How did she reach the freezer? She's a short four-year-old."

"What are you talking about?" Phoebe asked.

"I don't know," I said, scratching my head.

I couldn't have *imagined* Mom bought that ice cream. I *know* she did.

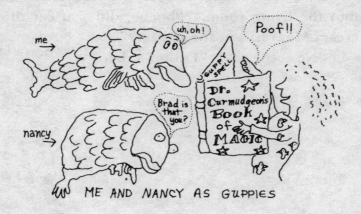

ME AND NANCY AS GUPPIES

CHAPTER

12

On the way to school Tuesday, Julie Bugle asked how things were going with the magic spells.

"Last night Phoebe tried to turn Nancy and me into guppies," I said. "Then she was going to shrink our heads and sell them as souvenirs. She was going to set up a booth at West Towne and sell them," I exclaimed.

"How great," Julie said. "Don't worry, Brad. I'll buy yours," she assured me.

"She made two quarts of ice cream disappear from our freezer," I said.

"Sure," Julie said, laughing. "I can make ice cream disappear too." She rubbed her stomach.

After school I went over to Martin Blue's house. We are doing a social studies project together. It's an Indian village. Martin is a possibility friend. I had never been at his house before. I don't know, though.

MARTIN IS A POSSIBILITY FRIEND

We don't have too much in common. Martin likes to play soccer. The only thing we have in common is the same things strike us funny.

We laughed a lot and didn't get much done on the village. We mostly threw clay at each other. I would like to do a project like that by myself. I would work for hours on research and make everything accurate. But the teacher wants us to work with another person. She thinks it's important. I don't know why when all we'll do is be goofy and make a dumb village.

After Nancy's bedtime Phoebe and I went right to *Dr. Curmudgeon's Book of Magic*.

"Let's do something crazy tonight, Brad," Phoebe said. "Let's conjure something for me. Like," she said, her eyes glistening, "a boyfriend."

"But you have a boyfriend."

"Not now. I broke up with Harvey."

"Who's Harvey? The last time you were here your boyfriend was Tim."

"Oh," Phoebe said, thoughtfully, "I'd forgotten about Tim. But I don't have a boyfriend now, so let's try casting a spell."

She thought it would be fun. I thought it sounded dumb. Phoebe found the page. I watched her as she began to read the spell. She had on an orange-and-pink-patterned pants outfit with bright blue birds on it. Her frizzy curls encircled her face. She was sort of pretty. I knew I really liked her. I knew that. I don't think there are many baby-sitters as nice and as fun as Phoebe.

> *"Liver spots on your tongue,"* she read.
> *"Candy canes and chewing gum.*
> *Thrash, thrash, boil and bash.*
> *Swallow your teeth and light the flash.*
> *Pickle. Worm. . . ."*

Before she could finish the spell, the phone rang.

"Oh, darn, we better answer the telephone," Phoebe said.

It was my mom and dad calling long distance

from Bermuda. We woke Nancy up so she could talk to them too. Nancy kept saying, "There was a chicken on my bed." Then she handed the phone to me.

"Phoebe has a magic book," I told them. "She's going to turn me into a guppy. Help! She's going to shrink my head and sell it in a booth at West Towne."

"Sounds like fun," my mother said. "Now let me talk to Phoebe."

Phoebe assured Mom that everything was fine, that Nancy and I were eating and not constipated and we hadn't caught colds or anything. When we hung up, Nancy had to go back to bed, and Phoebe and I resumed our practice of magic with *Dr. Curmudgeon's Book of Magic*.

Phoebe began again the spell for a boyfriend.

> *"Liver rots your gizzard out.*
> *Put your hand in a pig's snout.*
> *One for cucumbers. Two for elephants. . . ."*

I interrupted her. "Is that the same spell?"

"Shush!" she said.

> *"Two for elephants.*
> *Boo. Bats. Wretched rats. SNEEZE."*

We sat quietly waiting for a boyfriend to appear We didn't feel the room shake or anything.

"I think you ruined it," Phoebe whispered.

"I did not," I whispered back. "Anyhow, it didn't sound like the spell you began before my parents called."

"Look for yourself," Phoebe said, handing me the book.

The boyfriend spell did begin with "liver." But so did the spell on the facing page. *That* spell was for a . . . *werewolf*! I got a funny feeling in my stomach. I handed the book back to Phoebe.

"You're right," I said, hoping she was.

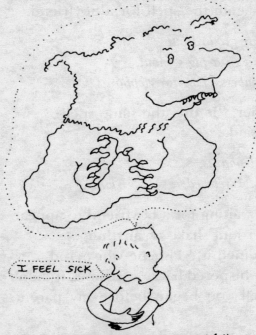

NOT THE WEREWOLF SPELL!!

There was a knock at the front door. Then the doorbell rang.

Phoebe giggled. "My new boyfriend!"

"Sure," I said. I went to the door. "Who's there?"

I called without opening it. My mother has strict rules about not opening the door at night.

"Delivery," some guy said.

I frowned. "Did we order something?" I asked Phoebe.

She shook her head no and headed for the door. It was a delivery guy all right. He had on a white uniform, and he held a brown paper bag.

two quarts of vanilla-fudge

NED

"The ice cream you ordered," he said.

I was just about to say, "What ice cream?"—when it hit me. "What ice cream?" I said anyhow.

He looked in the bag. Then he looked at Phoebe

and me. "Two quarts of vanilla-fudge," he said.

While Phoebe and I stared at each other, the delivery man opened the screen door and walked in. "Sign here," he said.

Phoebe looked at his paper. "It's for us. He's right," she said. "It's been charged to your parents' account at the drugstore."

"No tipping," the man said, even though Phoebe and I hadn't tried to.

hmmm

ME TRYING TO FIGURE OUT WHAT WAS HAPPENING

CHAPTER

13

I'm not sure how it happened. I think I went and sat down in the living room to try and figure out what was happening. I guess the delivery man helped Phoebe put the ice cream in the freezer and they were talking, and then all three of us were eating ice cream at the kitchen table.

Ned Zamm was his name. He looked about thirty

years old. He had red hair and he was big and strong-looking with bulging muscles and veins. Even his fingers had muscles. His muscles had muscles. My mother always said, "Don't open the door at night.

his muscles have muscles!

← even his fingers have muscles!!

NED ZAMM

Don't let anyone in the house. Don't talk to strangers." *We were having ice cream with one.*

"I've seen you in the drugstore," he said to Phoebe.

"I've seen you, too," Phoebe said. She was blushing.

At least, I decided, he couldn't be a werewolf. I don't think werewolves work in drugstores. The way

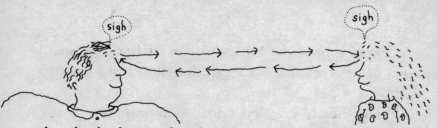

they looked at each other, it was possible Ned Zamm
was going to be Phoebe's next boyfriend.

He laughed real loud. Nancy woke up crying. Ned
sort of explodes when he laughs. While Phoebe went
to get Nancy, I asked him, "Do you believe in magic?"

He didn't say anything.

"Did you ever hear of *Dr. Curmudgeon's Book of
Magic*?"

"Is that a new rock group?"

"It's a book."

"Oh. I don't read many books. Other than school-
books. I spend my time working out at the gym and
the rest of the time I'm writing my master's thesis.
Would you believe I'm still a college student?" He
smiled apologetically. I looked at his white jacket.

"A part-time job," he said.

"Oh," I said.

"Eat your ice cream," he said. "Don't make
soup."

I like to make soup!

Phoebe brought Nancy to the kitchen. "A small bowl of ice cream for a treat and then right back to bed."

"Hey-hey-hey," Ned said. "What are you crying for, honey?"

Nancy wiped her eyes and looked at him. Ned tickled Nancy's chin. He grinned at her.

"You look good enough to eat," he said. "You look like the sweetest little morsel."

Nancy sniffed and wiped her nose with her hand. Ned held Nancy's arm out over the tablecloth. He shook salt and pepper on it. Nancy and I watched, fascinated.

"Now this little arm would really be tasty," he said. He opened his mouth and we saw *all his teeth!*

I jumped up, hysterical. I ran to Phoebe, who was behind the counter. "He's going to eat her. You cast a spell for a werewolf! We've got him and he's going to eat Nancy!"

Phoebe dropped Nancy's dish of ice cream. We both ran to the table.

Ned was smiling and Nancy was giggling. She was all in one piece. Two arms. Two legs. One head One body. All parts accounted for.

"Look, I got her happy again," Ned said proudly.

Phoebe glared at me.

"So I made a little mistake," I mumbled, rolling my eyes. "Nobody's perfect."

Phoebe got Nancy more ice cream and Ned helped her clean up the mess on the floor. Nancy ate and went back to bed. It was also time for me to go to bed.

I lay there in my navy-and-white-striped pajamas. I could hear the clock chiming. I could hear Phoebe and Ned talking softly in the living room. I was still awake when Ned left. I called to Phoebe.

"Aren't you asleep yet, Brad?" she asked. She turned on a lamp and sat at the bottom of my bed.

"I'm tired, but I keep tossing and turning."

"Look, I don't want that book of magic to upset you," she said. She reached out and rubbed my forehead. "It is my entertainment for the children I babysit. You know I always try to have some fun."

"I know," I said.

"I'm sure there's a perfectly clear explanation for the ice cream. It's like getting your fortune told. If you want to believe badly enough, you make it come true yourself. A sort of self-hypnosis."

"I know," I said.

"With some of the things that have happened, I've jumped to conclusions too. But it's all explainable when we take time to think about it."

"I know," I said.

"So I want you to go to sleep," she said, putting her finger on my nose.

"O.k."

She stood up, turned off the lamp and walked into the hallway.

"Phoebe, it's so late and so dark. I was thinking about Hepzibah. I was wondering if when it gets dark, he still flaps or if he goes to sleep."

"I'm sure he sleeps," Phoebe whispered. "And you should, too."

"Good night, Phoebe. It was nice of my mom and dad to call tonight, wasn't it?"

"Yes," she said, "they miss you too."

I nodded in the dark. "I know," I said.

I rolled over and closed my eyes. I thought about Hepzibah, sleeping. *I wish you could fly away, Hepzibah,* I thought. *I wish I could fix your wing. I wish I could make you fly.* And then I went to sleep.

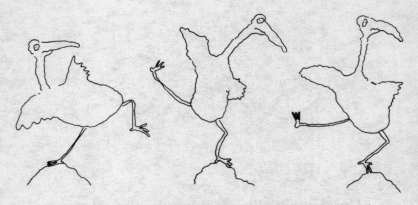

HEPZIBAH FLAPPING HIS WINGS TRYING TO FLY

CHAPTER

14

I woke up Wednesday morning thinking about Hepzibah. I couldn't get him out of my mind. I could picture him, up on that rock, flapping those wings like today was the day he was going to fly. My mind started filling up with ideas, ways to fix Hepzibah's wing. Maybe something could replace those flight feathers? Maybe I could devise something?

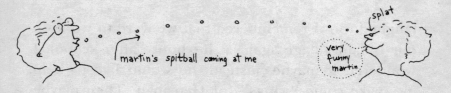

martin's spitball coming at me

splat

very funny martin.

I thought about it while I brushed my teeth. I thought about it while I dressed. I thought about it during breakfast.

On the way to school Julie Bugle told me a story about her funny parents, but I hardly heard. I was thinking about Hepzibah. I thought about Hepzibah all through social studies, math and band. I started putting my ideas into sketches during science. I thought about all the materials I would need. I knew we had art paper, string, a puffy plastic packing material in a box in the basement, some foam that our TV had been wrapped in when we moved here, old sheets, real feathers on an Indian war bonnet (from a third-grade Halloween party), glue, a couple kites (possibility of using two kites to brace around his wing), tin foil, plastic wrap—well, we had a lot of stuff in our house that might help Hepzibah. My mind spilled over with plans and excitement.

At the end of science class, Martin shot a spitball at me. I looked at him and he laughed, then I laughed too. I remembered that we were to work on our Indian village again at his house after school. I wondered if maybe, instead, he would like to help me make some "wings" for Hepzibah. Then maybe we could get Phoebe to drop us off at the zoo and Martin and I could make Hepzibah fly together. Then maybe we would decide to be best friends. I walked over to him.

"Hi, Martin," I said.

"Gowan, I can't work on the Indian village today," he said. "I have a soccer game."

"O.k." I said, sounding cool. But I felt funny. I hurried past him into the hallway.

Home from school, I set about gathering all the materials I needed from various parts of the house. I ran up and down the basement steps about six times and finally Phoebe asked, "What are you doing, Brad?"

"Nothing really," I said.

I have discovered that is the perfect answer. It seems to leave adults satisfied. They do not worry that you are doing something you should not be doing, like detonating dynamite, playing catch with a vial of nitroglycerin, planning a murder or throwing

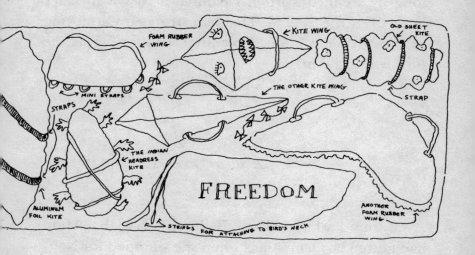

FOAM RUBBER
← WING

← KITE WING

OLD SHEET
KITE

MINI STRAPS

STRAPS

← THE OTHER KITE WING

STRAP

THE INDIAN
HEADRESS
KITE

FREEDOM

ALUMINUM
FOIL KITE

ANOTHER
FOAM RUBBER
WING

STRINGS FOR ATTACHING TO BIRD'S NECK

mud at the ceiling of your room. Usually when you say "Nothing really," they let you alone.

I worked solidly from three o'clock to five. I made eight different wings. One of my main problems was size. I couldn't remember how big his wing was. I made the wings about as tall as me. I had strings connected to each wing that would tie around Hepzibah's neck. I took a strip of white sheet, three feet long by six inches wide. I painted across it in black letters F R E E D O M. That had strings for attaching to the bird's neck too. I pictured it unfurling as the bird was in flight.

I found a huge plastic JC Penney bag that Mom had gotten last Christmas when she shopped for Nancy's and my toys and games. It held the eight wings nicely. I also put in two packages of uncooked popcorn. It was all I could think of to lure the bird to the fence, where I could then try the various wings on it. It seemed like a good idea too, to throw in Phoebe's *Dr. Curmudgeon's Book of Magic*. I would need all the help I could get.

I folded the enormous plastic bag over so no one could see what was inside. I went to talk to Phoebe.

"Phoebe, do you want to go to the zoo?" I asked.

"Not particularly," Phoebe said.

I blinked. She had to want to go!

"Don't you see I want to?" I said. "Phoebe, I have it all planned. I can make Hepzibah fly! Honest."

I told her all about it. I showed her all the wings and stuff and I figured when she saw how great they were, we'd jump in the car and go to the zoo. Phoebe didn't figure it that way. She was very nice, but she told me it just wouldn't work.

"Brad, dear, you have the best of intentions. But first of all, those animals at the zoo are not to be meddled with. And second, they are wild creatures and could probably hurt you if you got near enough to try a wing, which I doubt you could do. And what makes you so sure you know what is best for Hepzibah?"

"Well, I know he wants to fly," I said defensively. "You saw him flapping."

"But he's in Wisconsin, not Africa. How would he survive? He's used to being fed."

Phoebe sighed. Then she smiled. "You're a very nice boy, Brad. I know you are disappointed about this, but let's do something special tonight anyway. Let's go out for pizza. We'll have it instead of the dinner I was planning."

She paused, then said, "Darling, you're very sweet to have been working all afternoon for a big bird you hardly know. Hepzibah may be in the best place he can be, for all we know. So why don't we go for pizza?"

I had really figured Phoebe would be adventurous about this. "I thought you would think it would be fun," I said. "I wanted to let Hepzibah do his own thing like you want to do yours and it makes your parents unhappy. And like I want to do mine, but a nonathlete son makes my dad embarrassed."

Phoebe put a hand on each of my arms. She leaned close and looked at me for quite a while, as if she was going to say something important. But finally she shrugged, let go of me and said, "People are different from animals."

So we went out for pizza and on the way I saw Martin walking down the street. Phoebe stopped the car so I could ask him if his team won. They did. Then he said, "What are you doing?" and Phoebe asked him to come for pizza with us and he wanted to. We stopped at his house and his mom said he could.

When the pizza came, I pointed to the wavy things on top. "What's this? Did we order this?"

"It's an anchovy," Phoebe said.

"A what?"

"A little fish."

"The anchovy looks like it's still alive. It is! It moved!"

Martin laughed so hard he almost cracked apart. Then I picked up a mushroom.

"Oh, yum, yum, my favorite toadstool." I ate it. "Whoops, I forgot to make out a will." Then I died. "Agh-gha-aagh." It took me several minutes.

Martin liked that too. Maybe I went out of my way to entertain him. Maybe I'm trying too hard for a friend. It sort of makes me sick. Then Martin started throwing his pepperoni in Nancy's Coke when Phoebe wasn't looking. I think maybe we were too silly. I'm not sure.

silly drawing of the pepperoni my friend Martin threw in Nancy's coke

silly Martin

I had a little talk with Nancy that night after I read her a bedtime story. Her eyes were half closed and she looked like a fat dope addict.

"Nancy, you know what? Martin might be my friend. Do you like him aside from his throwing pepperoni in your Coke? I have a suspicion he's going to be a little boring. Some people need lots of friends. I don't. But I guess I do need one. I'll try not to goof it. I'll try to be interested in soccer. I'll do my best to think of funny things so he'll keep giggling. I wish friendship wasn't so hard. It seemed easier when I was younger."

Nancy began to *pouf*, which is what she does in her sleep.

"And another thing. I think I'm getting too big to walk to school with Julie Bugle. I'm going to avoid her tomorrow, even if it means I'll be late for school."

I tucked Nancy's covers in.

"Boy, Nancy, I think I really miss Mom and Dad. I'll be glad when they get home, won't you?"

I went to the living room and found Phoebe trying on the wings I had made for Hepzibah. She had the Reynold's Wrap wing on her right arm and the kite wing on her left. She asked me to tie the strings around her neck.

"Then I'll help you get into your wings," she said.

"What are we going to do, go trick-or-treating?"

"Fly! We're going to fly!" Phoebe said.

So we got dressed in the wings, and looking like two people-birds, we jumped off our front porch stoop and flapped as hard as we could. Neither one of us got airborne, but we had a fun time trying.

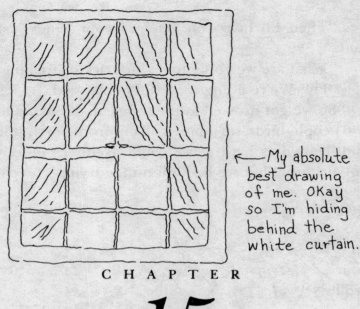

My absolute best drawing of me. Okay so I'm hiding behind the white curtain.

15

Thursday morning I hid behind the white curtain at the window in the laundry room. I wanted to see Julie Bugle going to school so I could avoid her. But when she walked to the rail fence and climbed over it, this irresistible urge made me open the door and call to her.

"Hey, Julie, hi."

"Hi, Brad," she said. "Walk with ya."

When I caught up to her she was smiling.

"You'll never believe what happened at breakfast this morning," Julie said. "My mother made a confession and we almost died laughing. She bought a little turkey last week and she's kept it a secret from us, can you imagine, for a week? A real live turkey! She keeps him in a cage by the firewood, but he got out and we saw him pecking at the door wall, trying to get in! When we discovered him, Mother was laughing so hard tears rolled down her cheeks. Then she told my father that in two months he has to kill it for our Thanksgiving dinner! My father was practically rolling on the floor laughing."

"Is your turkey white?" I asked. "If it is, I think I've seen it."

"You did? Why didn't you tell me?" Julie said.

"I didn't know it was yours. And I didn't know it was a *turkey* when I saw it on my sister's bed."

After school Martin and I worked on our Indian village, which is to say we threw clay at each other and giggled. Our Indian village is going to be the *world's worst*.

Walking home from Martin's, I saw Mr. Sonderman get off the city bus. I guessed he was coming home from work, because he was all dressed up in a business suit. I was going to say hello when he suddenly sat down on the curb and burst into tears. He was shaking and crying and holding his stomach.

"Are you all right?" I asked, but he didn't seem to hear.

I ran to the Sonderman house and rang the bell. Mrs. Sonderman came to the door.

"I think . . ." I said and pointed to the bus stop.

Mrs. Sonderman ran out, calling Gray. He stepped out of the house and looked down at the bus stop. Then he looked at me.

"Thanks, Brad," he said.

"O.k.," I answered, shrugging my shoulders as if it was nothing.

I walked slowly home, kicking pebbles along the sidewalk.

Phoebe said we better clean up the house because my parents would be arriving the next day. I was in charge of the vacuum. Phoebe dusted and scrubbed.

drawing of Nancy flushing six times ←

Nancy flushed the toilet six times in a row. She thinks she helps that way. Then I jogged around the block so I could tell my mother that I had. It was exciting to think about them coming home.

Phoebe took us to a seven-o'clock Disney movie. When we got home it was already past Nancy's bedtime, and my bedtime too, so I just read her a few rhymes from Mother Goose. She didn't mind. She goes to sleep fast.

"Nancy, it's been pretty much fun with Phoebe, hasn't it? I mean, aside from the fact she wanted to turn us into guppies and make us live in fishbowls for the rest of our lives. And I discovered it's almost as much fun to flap your wings as to fly. And sometimes making a dumb project with another person is better than doing it yourself and getting an A. Of course I may feel differently when I see my report card. Oh well, we made it through the week and tomorrow Mom and Dad will be home and we'll be back to normal."

I turned out Nancy's bedside lamp. There was moonlight on her pillow. It sort of gave her a halo. "You're a great little flusher," I whispered.

Report to Parents
Nancy and
Brad were
very good!
phoebe

When I got in bed, Phoebe came in my room to talk.

"My report to your parents will be that you and Nancy were very good children," she said. "You two are my favorites, you know. Some children I baby-sit are impossible brats. But you and Nancy are just plain nice and I like you very much."

"We like you too," I said.

"You'll come visit me at my shop, won't you?" she asked.

"O.k."

"And you'll take the dead leaves off Bill and give him a drink once in a while?"

"I will," I promised.

"Now, I can't find *Dr. Curmudgeon's Book of Magic*," she said.

"It's in the bag with Hepzibah's wings."

"I'll need it to keep the next children I baby-sit amused," she said. "Better go to sleep. I'll see you at breakfast."

"Good night, Phoebe," I said. "Oh, if you want

you can also take Hepzibah's wings. The other kids you baby-sit might want to practice flying."

"What a great idea," Phoebe said. She put her finger on the tip of my nose. "You are as generous as the newspapers say you are," she teased. "Now, really truly good night."

She turned out the light. I heard her walk toward the living room. I heard Pep come into my room and crawl under my bed. Soon he was snoring.

After breakfast Friday, Phoebe shook my hand and said good-bye. I think she wanted to hug me but thought I was too old for it. I wouldn't have minded. I kind of like hugging.

And yeah, I walked to school with Julie. I guess I'm not too big to walk with her. Besides, how could I start the morning without hearing about the Bugle kitchen-table hysterics—the laugh-a-minute family.

In school we started our electricity classes and Nelson Gammon almost got zapped into eternity because he didn't listen to the teacher's safety rules. Other than that, school was pretty dull. Martin thought I was going to work on the Indian village that afternoon, but I said, "Heck no, my parents are coming back from their trip." I had told him the day before, but I guess he forgot.

I walked home as fast as I could, even running part of the way. My mom and dad were glad to see me, too. They didn't care how old I was, they hugged me anyhow.

we missed you

"So, what's been happening?" my father said.
"Well, Howard Cosell called," I said. "He wants

to know if I'll box Muhammad Ali on *Wide World of Sports*. And Phoebe took us to the zoo and a movie and stuff."

"Was Nancy good?" my mother asked.

"Yeah, she was pretty good," I said. "Of course, she screamed when she saw the turkey on her bed."

"Sounds like you had fun," my mother said.

Then Mom and Dad told me all about Bermuda and eating lobster sandwiches for tea and riding the motorbikes and the colors of the water and the danc-

ing and how the people of Bermuda speak veddy proper English.

"We had such a marvelous time," Mom said. "We want to go back."

"If we can get Phoebe Hadley to baby-sit again," my father said.

"Phoebe Hadley?" I said, with my hands on my head and a faint look on my face. "Not Phoebe Hadley. Anyone, but not Phoebe Hadley. Do you know she was going to take Nancy and me on a mountain-climbing expedition to Mount Everest? Do you realize we had ice cream one night and she invited a werewolf to eat with us? Please, anyone, but not Phoebe Hadley." I collapsed into a heap on the floor.

"Oh, you got the ice cream?" Mother said. "Good. I think I'll call Phoebe tomorrow and set up next spring so we're sure to get her."

I ran to my room clutching my neck. "Oh no, not Phoebe Hadley. Promise me. Anyone but Phoebe."

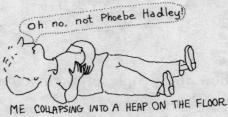

ME COLLAPSING INTO A HEAP ON THE FLOOR

DRAWING OF ME CLUTCHING MY NECK

Secretly, I was wondering what her hobby would be when next spring rolled around.